The Adventures of

Tulip

Birthday Wish Fairy

Dearest Henrie —
May every last one
of your wishes
come true.

love —
B

Written by S. Bear Bergman

Illustrations by Suzy Malik

flamingo Rampant
flamingorampant.com

Tulip

the Birthday Wish Fairy was late getting to work as usual. He always tried to be on time, but somehow something always happened. That morning it was a problem with his shoelaces. Shoelaces can be tricky things, you know.

When he arrived at the Wish Fairy Worldwide Headquarters, Tulip put away his umbrella, and opened the morning's Birthday Wish box. His job was reading the wishes of every child in the United States and Canada who had turned nine, and doing his best with each one.

Tulip hadn't been a Birthday Wish Fairy very long. His old job had been as the Fountain Wish Fairy at a fountain in the middle of New York City. It was nice spending all his time with child wishes. Sometimes grownup wishes were kind of boring.

Wish Fairy Headquarters

Going through the box of wishes, Tulip started arranging them into groups. An armful of wishes for new bikes and dolls and treehouses got a heavy sprinkle of high-grade fairy dust. A smaller pile of wishes to have a new baby brother or sister got dipped in Wish Fairy Bubbles, so they would travel up to where those kinds of decisions were made.

Another big stack of wishes from kids who did not want a baby brother or sister were sent to the Wish Wash. There they had the sad part washed off, so they could turn into the nice wishes they are underneath. Those wishes are really the wish to still have the love and care of their parents; to still be important.

The last big batch were the wishes to be taller or shorter, skinnier or fatter, blonder or darker-haired, less freckly or more freckly. All of those wishes were smiled at very nicely for fifteen whole minutes, so the children who wished them would feel better. The kids who wish them aren't really as different as they feel when they wish.

Tulip then picked up the sad and scary wishes, from kids whose lives were very hard. For the rest of the morning he read them. Birthday Wish Fairies are limited in their powers. They cannot do the things these children were asking them to do — make Moms not be sick anymore, make Dads stop hitting, make money come or trouble go away. Those are big jobs.

But Tulip brushed the brightest Wish Paint he had on each one, shining some Wish Fairy Light into each child's life so they could feel a little better. Every one of them would find a heads-up penny or a four-leaf clover, or someone would bring them a slice of cake or an ice cream cone, or they would see a bright butterfly or a songbird. A little something to lift their spirits. A little Birthday Help.

After that, Tulip had some lunch. He also got a slice of cake, with a scoop of sparkles on top. The scary and sad wishes were the best part of the job, but also the hardest. Sometimes he needed two slices of cake, if that pile of hard wishes was really big that day.

Luckily, the Wish Fairy Worldwide Headquarters understood what their Fairies needed. They kept plenty of sweets, treats, and shiny things around so the Wish Fairies could stay bright and shiny. And Wish Fairy Huggers were always around, to snuggle any Wish Fairy with a case of The Glum.

With most of the wishes sorted out, Tulip turned to the last small stack, about the size of a sandwich. He read a wish for a mean teacher to get nicer, and that one he dipped in Confidence Cream, so the child who wished it would find some courage to believe in herself.

For most of the afternoon Tulip read these wishes, until he came to one he had never seen before. A wisher in New York named David, had wished on his candles to be a girl named Daniela. Tulip had never seen this wish before (like I said, he was new) and he didn't know what to do with it. He thought and he thought. Then he looked at his Wish Fairy Rule Book, and found a rule for Wishes: Gender Change. The rule said:

Beauty In All Things, Jeff
Getting O
e Glums, Plum
Wish Fairy Rule Book
Solving Unsolvable Problems, Zevster
Bravery 101, Bobby
Art of Hugging, Miss Hanne
Defying Gravity, Turner
A Recipe for Sweetness, Sarah JVS
Advanced Snuggling, Stanley
Fairy Gods-mothering, Kate
Generosity With Style, Calvin
Awesomeness, Ishai
Sparkling, Chris

Wishes: Gender Change.

Unusual and complicated,
but not weird or bad.

Treat this wish with care.

If you need help,
go and see
The Wish Fairy
Captain.

Tulip thought some more. Then he got out of his chair, raised his umbrella, and told it he needed to see the Wish Fairy Captain. In a moment, he was whisked off to the office of the Captain.

Wish Fairy Headquarters

Tulip explained the wish he had just read, from David who wanted to be Daniela. The Wish Captain nodded and smiled. She said "That is a very special wish indeed, from a very special little girl." Then Tulip said, "I'm sorry, Wish Captain, but I don't understand."

"Are you confused about whether she's a little boy, or a little girl?" the Wish Captain asked. Tulip nodded his head. The Wish Captain explained that sometimes, someone was born looking like a boy, but had the heart and mind and soul of a girl inside. Or they might be the reverse: the body of a girl, with the spirit and thoughts and feelings of a boy.

Tulip asked what people do when that happens. "Well," said the Wish Captain, looking serious, "it usually starts with us — the person starts wishing when they are very small. First they wish for their body to magically transform into what they want it to be. Then, they start wishing for other people to treat them as they want to be treated."

Tulip made a serious face. Then he asked the Wish Captain why some girls are boys inside, and some boys are girls inside? The Wish Captain, who normally knew everything, shrugged her shoulders. "Nobody knows. It doesn't happen overnight. They just always and always feel different, until they can change."

"So David is a girl inside," said Tulip. The Wish Captain nodded yes and said, "And we're going to help her. We start by calling her by the name she chose, Daniela. It shows we like her and believe in her. And then, as Wish Fairy, here is what you can do:"

"Dip her wish in Bravery Broth, so she can feel brave when people don't understand her. Then go to her house while everyone's sleeping, and bring a bag of Clear Sight Sparkles. Sprinkle the Sparkles on her whole family, so they can see her as she really is inside. Put Teaching Paste on everyone's toothbrushes, so they can help her teachers and doctors understand her. Then as you leave give her a special Wish Fairy Kiss, so she knows her dreams will come true if she believes in them."

Tulip smiled, and then he nodded his head. He felt important to get to do such a big job. He thanked the Wish Captain, told his umbrella to take him back to his office. He dipped her wish in Bravery Broth and got all his supplies together for the visit. He added some extra sparkles for luck, because sometimes luck is a nice thing to have, and got ready to leave for his important job.

When it was nighttime, Tulip told his umbrella to take him to Daniela's apartment. It was dark inside, and warm. He tiptoed around. Tulip sprinkled the Sparkles and squeezed out the Paste. Then he found brave small Daniela, fast asleep, kissed her and put extra luck in all her pockets.

Then even though no one had asked him to do it, he went to the windowsill and twinkled it 'specially, so all the wishes of the house would go directly to Tulip's chair at Headquarters. Tulip got into the Wish Fairy business to help children, and he wanted to see what else he could do. Then he went home, and had a long sleep.

The next morning, a little late again (his jacket moved all by itself in the night!) Tulip began his day all over again. The usual great pile of wishes awaited him, and he managed them all as he had been taught. He sent good feelings and brightness, confidence and care to children in Toronto and Tallahassee, Boston and Bristol, Springfield and Sioux Falls and Saskatoon. He did this all week, and the next week too.

Late in the day on Friday, after giving a wish to tell the truth more often a bath in Bravery Broth, Tulip was ready to leave. Just then, a new wish flew in his window. From the twinkling, he recognized it as a wish from Daniela's house. He took it in both hands, and read it very carefully.

The wish was from Daniela's mother, and her wish was for her child to be free of bullies. Tulip was happy with this wish. He had been afraid she would wish for Daniela to go back to being David. He smeared Confidence Cream all over her wish, so she would feel strong when she helped Daniela to face her bullies. Then he smiled to himself.

As the weeks and months went by, Tulip did his regular job. He also kept his eyes open for wishes from Daniela's family. They came in from time to time: a wish from her dad that he think up new things they could do together, since he'd never had a daughter before. Another wish from her mom, for help being calm when she had to go talk to people at Daniela's school.

At first Tulip was upset by a wish from her two brothers, who wished that they could all move far away. But soon he understood that their real wish was that they live someplace no one had ever known Daniela as a boy, so things could be easier for her. Then he liked their wish a lot better. He sprinkled it with fairy dust, and made himself a little note to put some luck in their pockets too when he visited their house next.

The next time he visited was six months later. He brought extra Teaching Paste for everyone's toothbrushes, extra Clear Sight Sparkles for all. Daniela was asleep in her room, and he saw that it was different in there.

Her old boy's ice skates had been replaced by pretty figure skates, and her soccer uniform was for the girls' team. The clothes in her closet had a lot more flowers on them, and a pile of headbands and scrunchies for her new longer hair sat on her desk. He gave her another Wish Fairy Kiss, and whispered to his umbrella to take him back home.

The next day at work, which he would have been on time for if his cinnamon toast had cooled just a little faster, he found a note from the Wish Captain. It asked for Tulip to please come up and see her at lunchtime.

Tulip was very worried about this. Had he done something wrong? He worried all morning while he sprinkled and dipped and painted. At last it was lunch time, and he took up his umbrella and went to see the Wish Captain. When he got there, she asked him why he was still granting wishes at Daniela's house, since it wasn't her birthday anymore.

BRAVERY BROTH

"It was such a big wish, and it seemed so important," Tulip said. "I wanted to be sure that such a brave girl and her whole nice family got all the help they could get." He said it with confidence, but his knees were shaking. He was afraid he was in big trouble.

The Wish Captain smiled at him. "Tulip, you have done a wonderful job. I know you enjoy being a Birthday Wish Fairy, but would you be willing to change jobs again? I think the special children who wish Gender Wishes need a special Fairy all to themselves. Tulip, I think you're just the Fairy for the job. Would you be our Gender Wish Fairy?"

Tulip smiled the biggest smile a Fairy had ever smiled. He said: "Oh, yes! I would love to!" And the Wish Captain made it so.

She also gave him some extra tools and potions to do his important new job. Extra-Strength Confidence Cream and Bravery Broth, to start with. A tiny wrench for opening minds, and wee small stones for slowing down tongues that are too quick to say mean things. A special Smart Remark Spray for specially-gendered children to know what to say when someone asks them rude questions, and a friendly fuzzy compass for parents to find their way to the right people to help their families.

Soon, Tulip spent all his time with Gender Wishes. He heard wishes from small boys who wanted to be gentle and quiet, and from young girls who wanted to play rough and yell. There were wishes from boys who wanted to dance (even though people said *only girls dance*), and girls who wanted to play football (even though people insisted *only boys play football*), and from all kinds of children all over the world who were just a little different.

Tulip also helped little boys whose families thought they were girls, and little girls whose families thought they were boys. He helped their grandparents and aunties, uncles and cousins, teachers and doctors to start seeing them just as they wanted to be. He visited them in the night and kissed them all on their precious little heads, so they would believe in their dreams and follow them.

Wish Fairy Headquarters

Tulip was the happiest Fairy at Wish Fairy Worldwide Headquarters from then on. All the wishes he worked on didn't come true, but he always did his best. And so did his wishers, little and big, which is all any Wish Fairy ever really wants.

Tulip is a busy Wish Fairy indeed, and can't get to everyone's gender wishes right away. If you're a parent/caregiver or other involved adult and you'd like more information or resources for transgender/gender-independent kids – well, first of all, thanks. That's awesome. Second, check out Flamingo Rampant's booklist and other information: flamingorampant.com/familyresources

Teachers who would like to use The Adventures of Tulip, Birthday Wish Fairy to bring more gender awareness to their classrooms are awarded very sparkly cake, enthusiastically applauded and pointed at flamingorampant.com/schoolresources. We are working on developing curriculum guides to go with Flamingo Rampant books, and we will post them there for you once we're through.